THE BOY AT NO. 9
WHITLOCK
L. STEPHENSON

Copyright © 2024 L. Stephenson

ISBN: 9798340571571 (paperback)

All rights reserved. No part of this book may be reproduced or transmitted in any form or by any means, digital, electrical or mechanical, including photocopying, scanning, recording, uploading, posting, sharing, or by any information and retrieval systems, without the written permission of the author.

This is a work of fiction. Names, characters, places and incidents are the products of the author's imagination, or are used fictitiously. Any resemblance to persons, living or dead, is entirely coincidental.

Cover design by Chad Lutzke

Praise for Whitlock

"One of the most unique takes on coming of age horror I've read in some time. Sparse yet deep. Beautiful yet horrifying. I loved it."
– JUDITH SONNET
Author of Summer Never Ends

"A short, sharp, shock of a book...the horror and grief and palpable dread within make this a story to remember."
– ROSS JEFFERY
Bram Stoker-nominated Author of Metamorphosis
& Harvesting the Nightmare Fields

"Stephenson shows that horror isn't all about sending chills down one's spine; sometimes, it can be about moving the heart."
– REBECCA ROWLAND
Shirley Jackson Award-nominated Author of
White Trash & Recycled Nightmares

"One of the darkest coming-of-age horrors I've read. Grizzly and unrelenting. I wanted to look away, but I couldn't."
– KEV HARRISON
Author of Shadow of the Hidden & Below

"This book made my dark heart sing!"
– Y.M. MILLER
Author of You're Going To Die Here
& Marked for Sorrow

*I thank my dad
for giving me my love of horror movies,
and my uncle Mike
for introducing me to the works of James Herbert.*

*This book is dedicated to the
memory of their dad,
John Stephenson.*

Chapter One

Jillian Rose was dead. Dead even before her body swam with flame inside her vehicle. The steering wheel kissed her face on impact, firing her nose cartilage like an arrow through her brain.

The car roof peeled away, as if carved open by an invisible blade. Black smoke rolled up into the sky, carrying the woman's burning corpse along with it.

Its misty claws held her arms outstretched, her liquefying flesh plunging to the street below in sticky ribbons. The dark cloud poisoned every living thing it touched as it ferried her bones over trees, buildings and powerlines.

The oozing globes that shrivelled and shrank inside her blackened eye sockets sizzled with white fire as they madly searched rooftop after rooftop.

A single street sign, Whitlock, set alight beneath her hell path, dividing its name as it splintered in half.

She was closing in.

The charred soles of her feet touched down upon the road as she scarred her way down the center.

Lawns on either side were set ablaze by her presence. Lines of scorched dirt dragged across the grass as destruction followed her death march.

Jillian Rose came to a stop outside house No. 9, the second to last house before the lane reached a dead end. Its front windows shattered from the heat as she ascended the driveway.

Her fleshless fingers ground against the wall as she felt the bricks. And then, she started to climb.

She seized the windowsill of the first bedroom she came upon. The child inside shrieked in terror as her nightmarish complexion rose into view.

*

Her youngest screamed himself awake, floods of tears choking his cries of sorrow. Tears that would still be glistening on his cheeks by morning. Every morning since she left him.

Him, her youngest, Matthew.

Chapter Two

The summer of '96: that was when everything truly changed for the worse.

Twelve-year-old Matthew Rose snuck out of his father's house on that bright, warm Saturday afternoon. He would catch hell for it, but the boy didn't care. The reward was worth the risk.

First he waited at the end of the street for Ricky who lived on the next block over. They'd been best friends since they graduated to sippy cups. Next, Heather's house.

The pavement was hot beneath their bare feet as they stood outside melting under the afternoon sun. They kept themselves cool by flushing their throats with ice-cold water. Ricky snagged a fresh bottle from the fridge before he left. Its plastic skin crunched like trodden snow as they took turns holding it against their sweltering foreheads.

"Hiieee!" Heather's voice rang out as she skipped past them, sporting a lime green tank top and denim shorts. "Can somebody put this on my back for me?" she asked as she held out a royal blue bottle of sunscreen. "I'd do it myself, but I can't reach."

The boys coyly approached her as she laid herself stomach down upon the road, waiting for one of them to oblige her.

The two friends stood on either side of her like dueling gunslingers, their eyes entranced by Heather's naked lower back: its groove, its arch, its blemish-free skin. Not to mention the way it glistened in the afternoon heat. They exchanged an awkward glance. In that instant they knew the other felt something for the girl between them.

Was this what desire felt like?

Maybe.

Or perhaps something more than desire.

"Come on, guys," she urged them as she patted the curb, her lower back already slick with sweat. "Before I burn."

Ricky's hand shot up like an eager student. "I'll do it!" he exclaimed, crouching down like a crab upon Heather's backside.

Matthew grunted and swore under his breath, punching the air in his defeat. His toes curled in envy against the tar and broken stone as he watched the victor take up the bottle of sunscreen. Even the lotion itself mocked him as it emitted a loud fart noise when Ricky squirted a big splash across Heather's back.

"Thank you," she sighed gratefully.

"Here we go!" Ricky chuckled at his fallen opponent as he rubbed his hands together with excitement.

Matthew considered dragging the smug turd off of Heather. But what if he fought back? He didn't want to make it a thing. He didn't want them to know that he wanted it more.

It offered him some comfort when it became clear that Ricky had no idea what he was doing. He'd applied way too much, and it was taking far too long to absorb. The dope could only sit there and spread it aimlessly until the stuff was finally gone.

Heather was asleep by the time he finished. Stirring, she let out a long yawn as she got to her feet. A yawn that was more from boredom than anything else.

Matthew snorted with delight as he tried to contain his amusement.

Ricky glared at him and mouthed, "*Fuck. Off.*" when Heather wasn't looking.

That's when she turned to them both and said, "You guys wanna go down to the woods?"

*

Just beyond the preschool at the very edge of the village, the three friends climbed over the railings and helped each other drop down safely into the woodland stream below.

The stream itself was the center of a gully that cut through the terrain like a small valley, a quaint little pocket in the earth with steep slopes that ran up either side. The peak of one side was lined with the fencing of several backyards, while the other side flattened out onto a raised footpath that was a short stone wall's drop down into the country road that ran along next to it.

A small distance upstream, a single concrete drainage pipe descended from the row of houses above, opening out just on the edge of the water. Inside, the tunnel was large enough for a fully grown adult, while the outside was riddled with several clumps of fuzzy green moss.

Broken pieces of furniture littered the muddy shores on the other side: the remains of drawers, tables, cupboards, even the bottom half of a swivel chair. To a boy like Ricky, it was better than buried treasure.

"Who leaves all this stuff down here?" Heather asked as she gave the wreckage a frown of disapproval.

"The older kids," Matthew told her as Ricky rummaged through it all. "When they were our age, they used to bring this stuff down here, take it apart and build treehouses and stuff like that. My big bro was one of them."

Heather gazed at him attentively. "Treehouses?"

"Yeah." He nodded nervously.

"That's pretty cool," she said softly with a warm smile.

"Yeah…" Matthew's cheeks burned red with blush.

"Woo-hoo!" Ricky cheered as he held his discovery high, like the winning football team hoisting their trophy. "Guys! Look what I found! A skateboard!"

"That's not a skateboard," Heather pointed out immediately.

"I know that!" Ricky shot back, holding it out for them to take a closer look. "But I bet it'd be just as good. You could probably fit two people on here. How cool would that be!"

"*Pretty cool.*" Matthew shared a smirk with Heather as he repeated her words.

The board in Ricky's hands was soaked through, a piece of a corner broken off. One of its four caster wheels was missing, and several heavily rusted nails protruded from the other side, each of them bent sharply like steel claws.

"I dare you to ride it down there." Heather pointed to the concrete pipe, her smile glossy with mischief as the tunnel's mossy maw hungered for its next meal.

"Only if Matt does it with me," he insisted.

Matthew looked at Ricky and then at the dark mouth across the stream.

"Sure," he said with a shrug as he turned back. "What about those nails?"

"I can snap 'em off," Ricky told him. "They're rusty as shit, so they should come easy."

He planted the board upright in the mud and got to work, bashing each nail off in no time with a mango-sized rock he found nearby.

Before that hot Saturday afternoon, they had often marveled at the pipe from afar like a dangerous animal: better to just avoid it. Matthew got a good grip on the side as he approached the entrance and peered up into the tunnel. There was no scent in that place, not even from the water. Daylight would only help them so far up the first section of the pipe until the shadows engulfed them. Yet he could still make out the dimensions of a small room up there in the dark. But a room for what?

"Do ya think anyone lives up there?" Ricky uttered suddenly.

Heather jolted with a gasp of fright.

"Don't do that!" she scolded, swiping him across the ear.

"Hey!"

"Just get going already." Matthew shoved Ricky ahead of him and then followed him in. The climb was slow and uncomfortable, but it wasn't as wet as he had anticipated, nor was it as slippery. The most they had to be mindful of was a slim trail of twigs, dead leaves and dirt that wove its way down the center. And although they crept higher into the pipe, they never lost the light. The shadows he had seen from below must have been a trick of the eye, or perhaps even a trick of the mind.

Eventually the tunnel opened out into a small square room that gave them enough space to stand upright as well as side by side. Steel bars led up the wall to their left like rungs on a ladder to the inside of a manhole cover in the ceiling. Matthew gazed up at the ring of light that flickered down upon them as the sun shone through the trees above ground.

Straight ahead of them lay another tunnel mouth. This one was pitch-black, as if there was nothing inside. No life. No anything. Just darkness. The very sight of it gave them both a chill.

What was that place, really? What kind of creatures dwelled inside it? The woman from his nightmares? The one who looked like his mother but wasn't. He turned away from the dark mouth before his imagination began to draw shapes of monsters and horrors that weren't there.

The two friends didn't dare mention it or go any nearer to it. They just knew that they each wanted to be away from it as soon as possible. And in that moment, their new three-wheeled skateboard was the answer to their escape.

"Okay..." Ricky sighed, a shiver on his breath as he laid the board down ready. "You get on."

Matthew dropped to his knees and crawled into position, steadying himself as the board trembled beneath his weight.

"Really? You wanna go headfirst?"

"Can we just get this over with?" Matthew snapped.

"Okay..." Ricky gritted his teeth and shoved him. "Sorry!"

"Ricky, you fucking PRIIICK!" Matthew screamed all the way down.

Leaves whipped and dirt pelted his face as he went. The board hit the bottom with a wet slap, sending him rolling into the stream.

Heather leapt aside just in time, but couldn't outrun the resulting splash. She giggled at Matthew as he sat there, ass in the water.

Chapter Three

Matthew made it to the foot of the stairs before he realized he'd left a watery trail of footprints on the carpet, from that bottom step all the way back to the front door.

"Shit!"

The boy tore off his clothes where he stood and bolted into the kitchen with the bundle in his arms, careful not to spill another drop.

He returned in a fresh pair of shorts, paper towels in hand and dropped to his hands and knees, dabbing at the wet stains as fast as he could.

"Come on!"

His arms ached as he rallied to clean the entrance hall, when he heard the clicking of a lock from the turning of a key.

"Oh fuck..."

The door to No. 9 Whitlock crashed open.

A figure lurched through the doorway. It collapsed to the floor with a grunt. The body of Gordon Rose laid still upon its back.

"Dad?"

Matthew listened for a sign of life. He heard none. *Was he dead? Had he finally drowned in his own stinking vomit?* What a thought for his own flesh and blood to have, as he stood at his father's feet.

The soles of his guardian's boots were caked in clumps of grassy dirt, gravel and animal shit. As much as the putrid stench of fresh feces sickened him, he knew it would be no match for the boiling aroma seeping out of the man's horrendous trap.

If he were still breathing, that is.

The boy stepped alongside the body, grasping the wall for balance. He leaned in as far as he dared to go. Did the nostrils flare? Did the chest rise and fall? He couldn't tell. It was too dark in there. He reached for a light switch.

Two bloodshot eyes snapped open below, darting left and right in their confusion. They quickly spied the shadow that loomed over them. Gordon bellowed as he reached out and clamped a hand around its ankle. It gave a yelp before its blurry form fell away.

"Fuck are you doing? You tryin' to fuckin' rob me?" The words retched forth in a gross dialect that only his son could understand.

"No, Dad..." a tiny voice whimpered.

Shapes shifted and changed violently before the man's vision as he felt swells of blood crashing around the inside of his skull. He hauled himself up, shredding wallpaper with filthy fingernails.

He tore into the small bathroom by the front door and dove for the porcelain bowl. Vomit gushed forth from between his yellowed teeth with a great gargling roar. He held onto the rim as tears burned his eyes.

Matthew remained close by, wishing he could run up to his room and sleep away his existence. He wanted to step out into the inviting night and run until his legs could carry him no further. He wanted to think of himself for a change. But he couldn't. He couldn't in all good conscience abandon his father – or anyone else for that matter – whilst he was in such a sorry state. Could he? He cursed himself for inheriting his mother's kind nature.

One day I will leave him to fend for himself. One day.

The bathroom door coughed open, kicked ajar by one of Gordon's gagging spasms. Chunks of shit-smeared mud flopped onto the carpet like fish ripped from the sea.

Meanwhile, the boy could have fled his own skin from the fright it had given him. From that moment on he couldn't control the nervous shakes that overtook his hands. He tried his best to slow the thundering of his heart, steadying his breathing with deep, long breaths until its rate came down.

Unintentional or not, his father constantly terrorized him with such things: screams, crashes, false alarms, scare after scare. He delighted in it. Delighted in never letting his own son enjoy a moment's peace. And whatever peace he could find, it was soon torn away from him.

As the heaving went on, icy air nipped at Matthew's fingers like the shallow stings of frosted hornets. He looked past the bathroom and realized the front door had been lying wide open the entire time. It had to be shut before the chill found Gordon. He moved quickly to close it or else bear the brunt of punishment that would come if he left it as it was. His fingers wrapped around the handle, and then he couldn't let go. But it wasn't because of the cold metal that clung to his flesh.

Standing in that open doorway, Matthew gazed out into the night. His feet may have been bare, but he would walk until they bled if he truly believed he would never find himself back there. Just for a few precious moments he allowed himself to forget this possibility. He didn't think about where he would go or who he would go to. He thought about the feeling of being in between: a free spirit moving through the darkness, unseen, untouched and unharmed by anyone or anything.

There was a sudden gust of wind.

No, not a gust, but a thrust!

Gordon's fist smashed the door shut, its blunt edge missing his son's face by barely an inch. He yanked the boy around and pinned him to the stained glass.

Matthew struggled to breathe as he felt his father's weight, his gravity crushing against him, the sickly-sweet taste of beer and cigarettes hot on his breath.

"Fuck do you think you're goin'?" the brute growled, scoring the boy's young flesh with those dirty fingernails of his as they wrapped the front of his T-shirt into a tight ball around his fist.

"Fucking let me go!" Matthew squealed as he tried to shake himself free, but he wasn't going anywhere.

His head snapped to the right. The stained glass split beneath the side of his face. The left side, the side that got hit, began to throb furiously, his father's wet knuckles still dragging themselves away from the boy's cheek.

It didn't matter where he struck him, there was always an untold agony that burrowed its way down to his bones and coiled around his heart like razor wire. This was his father. How could he do this to him?

As his face began to swell over, Matthew looked at Gordon with his good eye and promised himself, *one day I'm gonna fucking kill you.*

What a thought for his own flesh and blood to have.

* * *

It was a quarter to midnight when Matthew finally mustered up the courage to sneak into the living room. Gordon had been passed out in front of the TV for a solid hour, leaving the coffee table in its usual mess of corn chips, beer cans and pistachio shells.

Matthew crept to the far corner where he retrieved the cordless phone from its home next to the lamp.

It made a bleeping sound that stopped him dead.

Fuck!

He held his breath as he turned to his father. Judging from the way Gordon was drooling all over himself, he hadn't heard a thing.

The boy took the phone to the tool shed out back where he sat next to the glow of an electric lantern and dialed.

"Hey Eric!" Matthew beamed sadly.

"Hey, Matty," his big brother's voice yawned on the other end of the line. "You're calling pretty late tonight, little buddy."

"Don't call me that," Matthew groaned.

"I know, I know," Eric chuckled. "So, is the old man out cold?"

"Every night."

"He still giving you a hard time?"

Matthew lowered his head, bottom lip trembling as he repeated, "Every night..."

"I'm sorry about that, Matty," Eric sighed. "Do you remember what Mom used to say about rainy days?"

"No?"

"She used to say, 'Boys, look at that sky. It might be raining right now, but there's always a sun behind those clouds. You just gotta wait for it'."

Matthew switched off the lantern as tears rolled down his face.

"Matty? Are you there?"

Matthew didn't reply. He just sat there silently weeping in the dark.

His brother did his best to comfort him until he finally had to say goodnight.

As the line played the dial tone, Matthew caught a glimpse of something moving as it watched him from the corner.

"Mom?"

He snapped on the lantern, its cold blue light illuminating the corner of the tool shed.

There was no one there.

There was, however, an old sled, a relic from happier times, still busted up, left unrepaired from when it last graced the snow.

Happy relic or not, the electric lantern remained aglow until Matthew was ready to turn in for the night.

Chapter Four

Symes and his buddy, Wayne, lived in the lower part of the village, where the houses all blended into row after row of solid brick wall. Walls that kept the wrongdoings of the unfortunate hidden from the judging eyes and ignorant minds of the suburban neighborhoods and gated villas that overlooked them.

Their bare, lean upper bodies were red raw from a morning of wrestling, and as the day moved on into the afternoon, the boys found themselves a new game to play.

Symes swung the metal pipe first. It connected with the little ball of spines with a soft thud. The hedgehog rolled halfway across the wet surface of the alley before it came to a stop. Symes' lip curled up in a sneer of disappointment. The hog hadn't let out a single squeal.

"Is that it?" he said in disgust, like a spoiled child on Christmas morning.

"Do you think it's dead?" Wayne asked, tilting his head in fascination.

Symes flipped the creature over with a jab of the pipe. A drop of red glistened along the side of the poor animal's snout.

"Its nose is bleeding," Wayne observed.

"Really?" Symes took a closer look. He smiled. "It's eyes are wet. Is it crying?"

"Think so," Wayne replied, his eyes shifting. He had seen enough.

"Huh! Little pussy," Symes scoffed at both human and animal, tossing the pipe aside. "I'm bored already. Get rid of it."

Wayne's mouth fell open as he shot his friend a look of horror. He turned away before Symes could notice.

"Go on, get rid of it," he repeated. "The game's no fun if it doesn't scream."

Wayne drew back his foot, scrunching his eyes as he dreaded the ensuing kick.

"If you harm that precious little thing anymore," an old woman's voice came from over the wall in front of them, "I'll have both of you runts put down!"

Symes tapped his buddy on the arm before he made a run for it. Wayne picked up the metal pipe and followed. He looked back as he ran, watching the old woman emerge from behind the wall in her robe to rescue the injured hedgehog, an oven mitt over one hand, a dish towel in the other.

"Whatever, ya crazy ol' bitch!" Symes shouted back at her.

Wayne giggled like a mad clown as they rounded the corner at the end of the alley. There, Symes grabbed him by the hips and pushed him up against the bricks, mashing his lips into his.

"That was fun," Wayne said dumbly, gasping for breath while Symes allowed him a few moments of air.

"So, what do ya wanna do now?" Symes whispered in Wayne's ear before he travelled down to the side of his neck and started sucking.

"Fuck!" Wayne cried suddenly, beating him away.

"What?!" Symes barked, confused, furious.

He bared his fists, ready to swing, until he heard the soft rumbling sound coming from the road behind him.

He dropped his hands and watched quietly as three familiar kids from the suburban neighborhoods coasted down the street on their bikes.

"Do you think they saw us?" Wayne asked him.

"If they did," Symes sighed as he took up the long metal pipe, "we're gonna make sure they keep their fuckin' mouths shut."

"Oh my GOD!" Heather screamed through her laughter as she sailed out over the stream.

She clung to the rope swing as it carried her in a wide curve over the water while Matthew waited downstream with hands outstretched to catch her.

"Thank you, thank you, thank you!" she cried. Her arms wrapped around the back of his neck as he guided her feet back onto solid ground. "Okay. I am not doing that again."

Heather gazed up into the treetops with wonder and amazement at what it must have taken for someone to tie the rope in up there at such impossible heights. The rope itself was blue polypropylene knotted tight as hell around its seat, an old but sturdy bare tree branch.

On that balmy afternoon, she, Matthew, and Ricky were about a hundred yards upstream from the concrete pipe where the gully opened out onto much more levelled terrain.

"Ha! Told you you'd love it." Matthew chuckled as he set about helping her dismount from the swing.

Heather watched him thoughtfully as he leaned over to untangle the foothold twisted around her ankle.

"That's new," she said, pointing at the deep purple of Matthew's black eye.

He ignored her remark, trying his best not to hurt her as he pulled her foot free. Thoughts of his father's heavy knuckles mashed against his cheek made doing so much more difficult than he realized. He hated Gordon for that. But not as much as he hated himself.

"I think I saw her again last night," he told Heather before he found the courage to meet her eyes again.

"Your mom?"

"Yeah."

"Where this time?"

"Tool shed," he said matter-of-factly.

"What do you think she wanted?"

"Probably just checking up on me," Matthew said.

"Typical mom stuff." Heather smiled warmly.

He almost forgot to smile back as he had a new thought: how much he loved the person in front of him for never making him feel like he was crazy.

For a moment, all that could be heard between them was the sound of life in the woods: the trees, the earth, the water.

Their heartbeats.

"You call that a swing?" Ricky snatched the thing from between them. "I'll show you a swing!"

Unbothered, the two of them stepped aside to let their friend have his moment.

He bounded past them with the grace of a polar bear, his strides becoming greater and bouncier as he prepared to take flight. Then he kicked a tree root. His arms flailed wildly as he became prematurely airborne.

"Shiiit!" he screamed as he plunged headfirst into the stream.

Matthew and Heather doubled over, choking on their own laughter, their teardrops catching the sun's rays as they fell to the dirt.

Ricky erupted from the water in one leap. His clothes made a wet slapping sound as he tried to shake himself dry like a wet dog returning from a walk in the rain.

"That'll teach you for last time," Matthew coughed through his hysterics.

"Yeah, yeah, yeah," Ricky grumbled as he trudged out of the stream. "Fuckin' prick..."

His head turned to the sound of a snap and a snigger.

"Guys, shut up!" He waved as he called to them. "I heard something."

"Grab her!" Symes cried as he and Wayne sprang from their hiding place.

"Come here, slut!" Wayne sneered as he bolted straight for the girl.

THE BOY AT NO. 9 WHITLOCK

Heather let out a pained squeal as the older boy grabbed the back of her neck. Matthew took a step to defend her, but her captor warned him away with a clenched fist.

"*Try it*," Wayne dared him.

"Hello faggots," Symes began as he strode between them, carrying the long metal pipe like a bat. "We're gonna play a little game called 'Do As I Say, or I Hit This Bitch's Head Like A Fuckin' Baseball'. Everyone got that?"

Matthew shared a look of worry with Ricky before he muttered their reply, "We got it."

"Okay." Syme's gaze led them to the top of the steep slope behind them. "I want you two to get on that one, at the same time."

On that slope was the other rope swing. As long as you held on tight, it would carry you out over a thirty-foot drop. And there was nowhere safe to land if you lost your grip.

This particular swing was something of an urban myth to the kids in the village, and Symes knew this. Just ask any of them. Guaranteed they had a friend of a friend who'd broken an arm or a leg trying to ride the thing. Matthew had tried it once. It certainly lived up to its reputation, because when it comes to a kid's imagination, swinging out over a thirty-foot drop? You might as well have been swinging out over the deepest ravine.

Only wide enough to carry one person, the two friends quickly decided to swing out face to face, making it easier for one to catch the other should they start to fall. And so Ricky lifted his feet as Matthew gave it a running start and kicked them off out over the drop.

Symes threw the first rock.

It was a lucky near miss for the boys as it zoomed past Ricky's arm.

Symes threw a second rock, harder this time.

He missed again by a couple of inches.

"Stop it!" Heather yelled at him.

"Shut your mouth, you fucking hog!" Symes snorted at her, furious as he took up the metal pipe. "Dodge this one, fuckin' fairies!"

Symes let out a maddened battle cry as he sent it spinning up through the air.

There was a loud *CLANG!* as it chopped Matthew across the back of the head. Both he and Ricky fell from the swing together, but only one of them was still conscious when they landed.

* * *

Eric Rose was studying at the university library when his roommate tracked him down to let him know about the call he'd received from the hospital. A short car ride later, he marched past Heather and Ricky sitting in the waiting area as a nurse with a clipboard led the way.

"What's up, little buddy?" he said as he appeared at the door to the examination room.

"Hey!" Matthew's face lit up through the pain.

"Hey Matty!" Eric smiled as he wrapped his arms around his little brother, lifting him off the exam table.

"What are you doing here?" the boy asked after he landed back down.

"Don't you know?" Eric folded his arms across his chest as he leaned back against the opposite wall. "I've been your emergency contact since you broke your arm last summer. So, what's going on here?"

"They asked me some stuff, checked my vision, and now I'm just waiting to get X-rayed..."

Tears found young Matthew's eyes. He couldn't stop them, though he tried his best to hold them back in front of his big brother, but it was impossible. Now that he was here with him, he felt a safety, an inner warmth that made his soul feel at ease.

"You okay, little man?" Eric bit his lower lip as he focused on the black eye.

"Yeah..." Matthew's mouth trembled as he lost his breath. "I'm just really glad to see you."

"Hey, hey." Eric held his little brother as he wept into his shoulder. "I'm here. I'm here. You're going to be alright, little buddy. Everything's going to be alright. There's always a sun, remember. Just like Mom used to say. No matter how dark that sky gets, there's always a sun behind those clouds. You just got to wait for it."

"Okay kid, you're up!" said the nurse with the clipboard as she returned, pushing a wheelchair. "Let's go get you X-rayed."

Matthew looked at Eric sheepishly as he got into the chair. "Are you going to stay?"

"Yeah, you bet," his big brother nodded reassuringly. "I figured we'd hang out later. Catch a movie or something."

"Excellent!" Matthew cheered, beaming from ear to ear as the nurse wheeled him out of the examination room.

Eric exhaled heavily as he retrieved a handful of paper towels from the dispenser by the door. The door where Gordon Rose suddenly appeared as his eldest son dried the fallen tears of his youngest son from his shirt.

Looking up, Eric immediately took a step back.

"Dad..." he gasped soundly as the paper towels fell to the floor.

"Hello, Eric." His father leered at him as he began to massage himself below the belt of his denim jeans.

* * *

The car radio read 11.30 p.m. when Matthew and Eric pulled up to No. 9 Whitlock.

Despite having gorged themselves on hotdogs, candy, nachos and Slurpees at the movies, the brothers couldn't resist grabbing themselves a couple of cheeseburgers with fries and shakes on the way home. And although this made them extra late, Matthew didn't care. It had been so long since he knew what a full belly felt like.

He couldn't even remember the last time that someone spoiled him.

"This was the best," he sighed contently as he laid back in the passenger's seat. "I had the best time."

Eric smiled over at his little brother, but it faded the moment he saw that black eye again. He had to stare at the thing all night, and each time he did, his heart broke that little bit more.

"Listen to me, Matty, because this is the best piece of advice I'm ever going to give you," Eric said cryptically. "If Dad ever, *ever* does anything more than hit you, don't tell anyone, because they'll just laugh. And they won't believe you. When the time comes, you'll have two choices. You either run, or you fight back...*hard*."

"What would you do?" Matthew failed to hide the nerves in his voice as he asked the question. He knew exactly what he wanted to hear, and yet somehow he was still afraid of the answer.

"I already made my choice, I ran," Eric admitted before he met his brother's eyes. "But if I had to make the choice again...I'd kill him."

*

"*You're* late," was the first thing out of Gordon's mouth as Matthew appeared in the doorway of the living room. The man didn't even take his eyes off the television, a can of beer clasped in one hand, a smoking cigarette nestled between the nicotine-stained fingers of the other.

The boy had no defense, he knew full well he'd blown his curfew, to smithereens.

"Ashtray," his father uttered.

It wasn't a request, nor was it a question. It was a command.

"Dad, no–"

Boom! The coffee table shook beneath the heavy heel of Gordon's boot.

"Ashtray!" the man bellowed.

Matthew obeyed his order, scurrying into the room and sitting down on the floor at his father's feet, where his legs always had to be crossed, and his head always had to be turned to the TV. He listened to the hiss of Gordon's beer as it fizzed away inside the can. He used its noise to calm the pounding of his heart, to un-shake the shaking of his breath, but mostly, to see him through what was about to happen next.

Without ever acknowledging his own son with his gaze, Gordon Rose took a long, deep drag of his cigarette, its tip burning orange bright, and then he flicked it as he used the top of Matthew's head as a human ashtray, again.

* * *

Just before sunrise, Katherine Wilkinson took her Jack Russell Terrier, Bennett, for their usual early morning walk into the woods. Even through the thickness of the treetops, the cloud-covered sky cast a peculiar shade of gray over everything. Even the lush summer greens of the leaves appeared pale and faded.

Bennett began barking before Katherine even knew anything was wrong. For some strange reason her little boy wouldn't play fetch with her, wouldn't listen to her commands, wouldn't even beg for one of his treats. Was it another animal? Bennett had always hated squirrels with a passion. It wasn't until he laid himself upon the ground and whined as he stared fixedly upstream that she finally realized it had to be something much more serious.

Unsure of what lay ahead, Katherine searched for a broken branch or a loose rock to protect herself with as she followed the dog alongside the gently running water. But before she could find anything, what they were looking for suddenly came into view, stopping the old woman in her tracks.

"Oh! Oh no..." she uttered sadly.

The body hung silently over the stream up ahead from one of the rope swings the kids from the village loved to play on.

Katherine sobbed as she approached the young man's body. Not because she was uncomfortable or afraid, but because she knew him. It was Gordon's eldest boy, Eric Rose. That family was never the same since the passing of his mother, Jillian. Such a lovely woman. And now this.

As she made her way closer, Katherine noticed something hanging across Eric's chest. It was a wooden sign, and upon it were four words, finger drawn in blood.

THERE IS NO SUN

*

In the impossible haze of what had happened, there was no time for Matthew to mourn. Before he and his friends knew it, their first year as high school students was just beginning. Their summer was over, and fall was finally here.

Chapter Five

There were no words Matthew could find to say how much he missed his brother Eric. And in the finding of no words, there was no Matthew. He had lost himself so completely that he could feel it, the great emptiness that had opened up within him. When he walked across a room, or along a sidewalk, he felt the air moving through him as if he were an apparition adrift in the land of the living. If Gordon's fists were to find him now, would they slam straight through him? The boy cared little enough to test out this theory, and, true to form, his father was only too happy to take out the grief of losing his first son on the one that was still breathing. From there, things only got worse.

Thanks in no small part to a combination of mediocre grades and a considerable lack of parental support, both Matthew and Ricky found themselves attending the very same piece of shit school as Symes and Wayne. From the moment they laid eyes on each other that first day in the main lunch hall, it was either run and live or stand and die. Ricky instinctively chose for them. "Run!"

They burst out into the school corridor to find a maze of student bodies on their lunch break, chatting away in their little clusters as they swarmed the place from end to end.

Ricky slipped out of sight, but Matthew was not so quick. Symes snatched the boy's shirt collar with clawed fingers and hurled him against the wall, pinning him into place like the latest edition to a butterfly collection. The older boy loomed in close, his face boiled to a reddish pink.

"Who'd you tell about the woods, asswipe?" His eyes blazed as he bared his jaws like a mad dog.

"I didn't..." Matthew turned his head away from the spit that sprayed from Symes' heaving breath.

His feet left the ground as Symes lifted him into the air and slammed him against the floor.

"Well somebody fuckin' did!" he sneered down at him, booting him hard in the side of his leg before he pushed his way back towards the main lunch hall. "Outta my fuckin' way, twats."

* * *

"Do you want to talk about what happened?" Christopher Hull asked from the other side of the desk as he sat upon the edge of the battered steel cabinet by the far wall of his office.

The high school counselor was a chinless oddity with shoe brush hair who never failed to appear dressed in the drabbest ill-fitting work clothes you'd ever seen. And although he only had one missing finger on his left, his hands were so big that it always seemed like more.

Hiding the swollen side of his face with the hood of a fisherman green raincoat, Matthew Rose looked out into the square garden enclosed within the long corridors of the school. The plot wasn't particularly well tended to. If anything, it appeared as if God had carved a tiny piece of land out of some far-off countryside and abandoned it there in that strange place to wither and rot.

In the center of that sad little courtyard was a lonely bench, a long-forgotten memorial perhaps. The boy couldn't help but imagine the woman from his dreams sitting there. Her flames would turn the faded wood to charcoal gray as her unearthly stare burrowed into him. Smoke would seep out of the patches of bare grass as the trees, bushes and plants combusted all around her.

Why did she look like that? he wondered.

She had appeared to him the night before. Awoken by the sharp stab of a whisper's hiss, Matthew opened his eyes to find his bedroom ceiling aglow with firelight as the cracks upon it drew the form of her face. The walls shook as she opened her splintering mouth to speak. She spoke only one word, his name, and then the dream was over.

Who was she? And what did she want from him? Matthew knew one thing for sure: she was not his mother.

"I can't make you talk to me," Hull said as he finally took a seat at his desk. "But you're going to want to talk to someone eventually. You're free to go, but you and I are going to keep this same appointment every week until you trust me enough to be that someone. Some things are too hard to talk about with your friends. And I can keep a secret."

The boy got to his feet. Resting the strap of his backpack upon his shoulder, he gazed at the counselor with a look of uncertainty.

Hull gave him a simple nod. "I'll see you next week, Matthew."

* * *

Heather and Ricky were waiting beneath the great oak that grew on the lane at the end of Whitlock when Matthew hopped off the bus two blocks down.

"I don't wanna talk about it," he said before either of them dared to ask.

"Did you talk at all?" Heather challenged him, but all she heard in response was the distant rush from the vehicles of daily commuters slicing through the air on their passage through their little village. "Did you say anything?"

Slipping his fingers into his pants pockets, Matthew's lips remained sealed as he squinted into the pale autumn blaze of the afternoon sun.

"Shit!" Ricky grunted as the three of them turned to the whir of bicycle wheels fast approaching.

Symes tore down the lane towards them, Wayne close behind. His legs pumping, his nostrils flared as his breath hissed through clenched teeth.

"You fuckin' squealed on me, faggot?" he cried with a bewildered rage as he dismounted.

His bike crashed into the great oak as he took his first swing at Matthew. He hit him square across the jaw. Not enough to take him down, but enough to double him over.

"Leave him alone!" Heather screamed. "He didn't do anything!"

Her protests went unheard as Symes went in with the second blow, sending Matthew scrambling over the road, his hands clawing at the ground to stay balanced.

Meanwhile, Ricky clipped Wayne's ear with a fallen twig from the oak and led him on a chase down Whitlock. Ricky was never much of a fighter, but at least his little distraction would keep the odds fair.

Symes ignored Heather's threats to alert the neighbor who lived on the corner as he took up a stick he'd found amongst a pile of fallen leaves. He made sure that she saw the delight in his smile before he turned to Matthew with his weapon raised high.

THWACK!

"No!" Heather cried as she ran back to them.

THWACK! THWACK! THWACK!

"What the fuck?" Symes hadn't moved a muscle, the stick frozen in his grip.

Matthew was hitting himself.

One after the other, he drove a set of knuckles into the side of his face, battering his head this way and that. Just the way his father liked to do it.

Neither Heather nor even Symes had ever seen the look that was in his eyes. They saw pain. They saw sorrow. They saw hopelessness.

And then they saw blood.

"Stop it, stop it, stop it!" Heather yelled as she threw her arms around him. "I'm not letting you go until you stop it."

He knew that if he tried again he would risk hitting her too, and he couldn't have that. He would never forgive himself. And so his trembling fists became hands again and his arms surrendered as he returned his friend's embrace.

Symes discarded the stick with a scoff and retrieved his bike from the great oak. "We'll finish this later, psycho boy."

"Go away, you jerk!" Heather held Matthew tighter, closer. "Get lost!"

Symes gave her the finger as he rode away.

Heather whispered softly into Matthew's ear, "I know you're not in the talking mood right now but...we're gonna need to talk about *this*."

The two of them sat together on the curb outside No. 9 Whitlock. Heather waited patiently by his side while Matthew could barely bring himself to look at her, or anything at all for that matter.

But then, as he watched the sun hanging low over the rooftops, he let out a long heavy sigh and said, "There's something I didn't tell you about the day Eric died." His voice tremored on those final few words. "Something I thought I'd never tell anyone."

Heather leaned against his shoulder and started to rub her friend's back as he began.

"I was home alone when I found out. The cops knew they'd find Dad at the bar. So they told him what happened, and that's when he called and told me.

"Someone found Eric's body in the woods. My brother... *My big brother* was dead.

"I went quiet. I stayed quiet for a long time. Then after a while I cried. But not just from my eyes. It felt like I was crying from everywhere, from every part of me. Like someone cut me open, and my tears were just draining out of me like blood. Maybe I really was bleeding because everything hurt.

"I guess that's why they call it heartache. Except it's not just your heart that aches, it's your entire body. And then I just fell apart. I couldn't speak. I couldn't breathe. Then I couldn't even stand up. I wasn't even strong enough to stop myself from sinking into a heap on the kitchen floor. This terrible feeling was just dragging me down. So I just laid there.

"After a little while I felt like I could move again. So I got back up, and the first thing I did was get a knife out of one of the drawers. It was small, but it was sharp. I remember watching Mom slice meat with it when she used to make us dinner.

"I was still crying when I put it to my wrist, and then I made the first cut...

"I don't think I made it even a quarter of an inch and I had to stop. I barely drew any blood at all. I didn't go deep enough. It wasn't much, but it hurt like hell. Way too much for me to keep going. I don't really know why I stopped. Maybe I was too afraid of what would happen to me after I'm gone. Life wasn't so great, so why would being dead be any different."

As Matthew's story came to its end, the hand that had been comforting him was now clasped over Heather's mouth. Her tearful eyes smiled at him as the hand fell away and squeezed his arm.

"I'm glad you're still here," she sniffed as she pulled out a hanky and dried her face. "You're still thinking about it, aren't you. That's why you lost it. You wanted him to kill you."

"Maybe... I don't know," he told her before he met her eyes and said, "I just know I don't want to be here anymore."

"Matt," Heather said with a hopeful smile as she took his hand in hers, "what if you could talk to your mom and Eric again?"

Chapter Six

Ricky leaned against a French stained mahogany dressing table scrunching his nose. Its surface glittered with crystals of all colors and several pieces of loose jewelry.

"Jeez, this house smells funky!" he winced as he watched Heather rifle through the highest drawer of a tall black chest that stood in the far corner of her aunt's bedroom.

Matthew smirked as he held back a chuckle.

"That's just my auntie's incense candles." Heather rolled her eyes at her friend as her searching fingers brushed aside a folded quilt. And there it was. "Found it!"

The boys huddled round her as she placed it thoughtfully upon the bed. The board was the color of old parchment paper with ink-like Celtic lettering. Each corner had a word: Yes, No, Hello, and Goodbye. Across the center were all twenty-six letters of the English alphabet, and below that was a large, five-pointed star, a pentagram.

"A ouiji board?" Ricky backed away. "What is she doing with one of those?"

"She and my mom used to play with it when they were kids," Heather replied as she gently dusted off the board. "Like when they had sleepovers with their friends. Mom told me one time it even caught on fire and flew across the room."

"Oh fuck that!" Ricky threw up his hands and marched for the door. "I don't like this at all."

"Shut up, Rick." Matthew shook his head at him. "Don't be such a wimp."

"Both of you shut up," Heather scolded them as she slid the board into her backpack. "Let's get out of here before my auntie makes us stay for dinner."

Slinging the pack over her shoulder, she quietly led them out to the landing.

"Did you find it?" a voice called from downstairs before she could reach the top step.

Heather's shoulders sank. "Uh, yes, Aunt Sheila," she answered as they all made their way down. "We were just leaving."

"Not so fast!" Heather's Aunt Sheila called from the doorway of her living room as she raised a hand to halt her eager young guests from making their quick escape.

Long turquoise nails tapped on the doorframe as bangles and bracelets of silver and gold jangled on her wrists. The woman wore a floor-length, purple silk dressing gown decorated with white flowers beneath a wild mane of frizzy red hair, icy green eyes and hoop earrings.

Behind her, the incense burned upon the mantelpiece, and in the corner to her left, an old episode of *The Jerry Springer Show* she'd recorded on VHS played with the sound off.

"If you kids are really serious about what you're doing, you're going to need an Earth line."

"An Earth line?" Heather asked her aunt as she slowed to a stop at the foot of the staircase. "What's that? I've never heard of it."

"It's the line that grounds the astral plane, and reinforces the protection the pentagram provides, making it so that only good spirits can communicate with you," Sheila explained as she guided them all into the living room. She plucked a book from a pile on her side table and presented to them the symbol upon its cover, a second pentagram, embossed in gold.

"All you have to do is create a straight line at the base of the star," she continued as she ran the tip of her finger between the two lowest points. "Do that and you will be safe from all harm."

"Okay," Heather nodded, looking from Ricky to Matthew. "We will."

"One last thing that you have to promise me that you will never do," the woman said cryptically, her fingers drumming anxiously against the hardcover of the book sitting on her lap.

"What is it?" her niece asked.

"Never invert the star on that line."

"Why?"

"Because the upside-down star is the shape of the goat, the horned one himself, Lucifer," Sheila told them as she flipped open the book to reveal a diagram of the creature she spoke of.

"The devil," Ricky uttered as he felt a shiver scrape along his skin with its cold claws.

Sheila nodded. "Only bad things come looking for you when you tempt Satan's eye." And with that she snapped the book shut.

* * *

Heather opened the very same book upon the floor of Matthew's bedroom as he and Ricky sat on either side of her.

"I feel much better about doing this with your auntie's book here," Ricky remarked as he let out a sigh of relief. "But when did she give it to you?"

"She didn't," Heather said, baring her teeth guiltily.

"I swiped it," Matthew confessed with a proud grin.

Ricky's relief vanished. "Oh great. Because nothing bad ever happens to people who steal things."

Matthew gave his friend a sniff of amusement before he glanced down at the handle of the knife he'd concealed in the front pocket of the hooded sweater he wore on that evening, the knife that he'd cut himself with. He didn't know why it brought him comfort to have it with him. Perhaps because its blade knew him in ways that no one else ever would.

The ouiji board sat in the center of them atop a small round table. Three lit candles were positioned around the board as the three points of a triangle. "To represent the Holy Trinity," Heather explained, "The Father, the Son, and the Holy Spirit," before she led them in reciting the Lord's Prayer, reasoning that they needed, "all the help we can get."

Ready to begin, Heather drew their Earth line beneath the pentagram with a piece of chalk as Matthew placed two photographs next to the board: one of his brother, Eric, and the other of his mother, Jillian.

"Okay, everyone hold hands," Heather instructed them. "And don't let go until it's over. Remember, we aren't finished until we've said goodbye to the spirits."

She looked to Matthew as he squeezed her hand. He thanked her with his eyes as he gave her a sad smile. She gave him a nod in return and then stole a moment for herself as she closed her eyes and took in a breath.

"We wish to commune with the spirits that have lived here in this house," Heather began. "Jillian Rose, we wish to commune with you. Your spirit is welcome here with us. We wish to commune with the spirit of Jillian Rose. Jillian, please hear us. Let us know you are present among us."

The three of them gazed around Matthew's bedroom as they listened for a sign.

They heard only silence.

Heather repeated the chant two more times. And two more times there was nothing.

She tried once again, this time with a different chant. "We wish to commune with the spirit of Eric Rose. Eric, your spirit is welcome here with us. We wish to commune with you. Eric, please hear us. Let us know you're here with us."

They waited again.

"I don't think this is working," Ricky finally spoke up.

"Quiet!" Heather scolded him. "Eric, can you hear us? Give us a sign that you're here with us. Eric?"

Matthew let out a sigh of disappointment, blowing out the candle nearest to him. Cursing under his breath, he grabbed the tiny box next to Heather.

"He broke the circle!" Ricky exclaimed.

"It's okay, we haven't made contact yet," Heather reassured him. "Matt?"

Hands unsteady, Matthew pulled a match from the little box and tried relighting the candle, his eyes fixated on the extinguished wick.

On the first strike, the match didn't light.

"Matt?"

On the second strike, he dropped it.

"Matt?"

And on the third strike, it snapped.

"Matt!"

Matthew kept his fingers clasped around the matchbox as he set it down on the table.

He knew the feeling of when there was a presence nearby all too well. It was like there was an invisible pull from somewhere inside him. He could never tell whether it came from his head, his heart, or his entire body, but it was there, drawing him towards it. In the quiet of that room, he felt no pull. No pull at all. What he did feel was loneliness.

"Guys," he said as he watched the grayish-blue smoke still rising from the blackened wick. "Maybe Eric can't hear us. What if it's true what they say about people who kill themselves? What if their souls really do go to hell? How can he hear us if he's stuck there...*forever*?"

"I don't know," Heather answered him honestly. "But I don't think that's true for a second. I don't believe God would do that to people. It doesn't sound right to me. Wherever he is, I think he's somewhere safe."

"Then why doesn't he say anything," Matthew sobbed as he lowered his head. "Doesn't he know I need him?"

"I'm sure he does." Heather reached over and rubbed his arm. "We'll keep trying."

As he looked down, the glint of the blade caught his eye. It had been waiting for him. It was there for him when he needed it the day Eric died. Perhaps that's why he believed it was the only thing that could help him now.

"Fuck this!" he grumbled as he reached across the board and erased Heather's chalk line with a swoop of his fingers.

"Matt, what are you doing!" Heather cried as he drew the knife. Her jaw dropped as he plunged it into the board and dragged its blade over the highest point of the pentagram.

"Matty, why'd you do that?" Ricky whimpered. He turned to Matthew and screamed. "Oh Jesus!"

His friend's eyes had rolled over white, his arms hanging limp on either side as he sat there perfectly still.

The room darkened as the candlelight shrivelled away into nothing, as if something had choked the oxygen out of the flames.

"Matt! Matt, are you okay?" Heather called to him.

"I'm okay," Matthew responded calmly. "I see something."

"What do you see?" she asked, sharing a worried look with Ricky.

"I'm outside on our street," he told her. "It's nighttime. Something heard us. Something that wasn't supposed to."

"Who heard us?"

"I don't know. But it's standing at the end of our street. I think it's looking at me... It sees me!"

"What's it look like?"

"I can't tell, it's too dark," he said. "But it's tall, like a giant. And its eyes... Its *eyes*–"

"I don't like this." Ricky grabbed Heather's arm. "Can we wake him up?"

Heather shook her head. "I think that's a bad idea."

"What the..." Matthew gasped. "It's floating towards me."

"Run!" Ricky yelled.

"I am!" Matthew yelled back.

"Don't let it catch you," Heather warned him as she placed a hand upon his knee.

"Okay, I've made it to the house," he told them.

"Make sure it can't get in."

"Shit, it's at the door!" he cried.

The room shook around them as a crashing thud came from downstairs. Heather snatched her hand back with a scream. Her eyes met Ricky's. They were wide with fright.

"What was that?" he stammered as he huddled against her. "I thought this was just in his head. Why are we hearing that?"

"Guys..." Matthew whispered sharply, "it's inside the house..."

There was a creak.

Then another.

And another.

"It's coming up the stairs!"

Ricky squealed as he shook Heather by the shoulder. "What do we do?"

She batted him away. "Stop that! We're here to talk to the spirits. So I guess we just talk to it."

Suddenly, the creaking stopped.

"What just happened?" Ricky looked to Matthew. "Did it go away?"

"No..." Matthew said quietly, turning to face them as his eyes returned. "It's waiting for us to let it in..."

Matthew looked towards the door. He froze.

"Oh my god..."

The thing he'd seen in his mind was standing there by the door, looking right at him. Its bony frame was as tall as the ceiling. Its rotten flesh was pitch black, like a starless night sky. And its eyes were wide and piercing. Their stare haunted him.

"It's here!" he cried as he flung himself backwards.

His friends screamed as the bedroom door burst open.

"What are you doin' in here?" Gordon's voice said from the doorway as he snapped on the light. His squinting eyes looked over the three of them, and then they found the ouiji board. "What the fuck is that?"

Gordon stomped into the room. "What the fuck are you doin' messin' around with this?" he pointed accusingly at the board, booting it across the floor.

"I'm sorry, I'm sorry, I'm sorry!" Matthew yelped as he tried to move out of Gordon's path, but the brute was too quick.

He slapped his son hard across the face, latching his fingers onto the boy's collar so that he couldn't escape. He started kicking, again, and again, and again. Every time his father kicked him away, he would yank him back to kick him some more.

"Mr. Rose, we're sorry," Heather bravely tried to intervene. "Please, we were just–"

"Shut your mouth, ya stupid little cunt!" Gordon barked at her.

Ricky hugged his arms around her and guided her away from him as she started to cry. The two of them sat on their friend's bed and waited for the beating to stop, afraid of what might happen to them all if they tried to call for help.

"Am I bleeding?" Matthew mumbled when it was over. "I feel like I'm bleeding."

Heather and Ricky sat by him as he lay curled up in the corner of the room.

"Nah, bud," Ricky said after he looked him over. "But it looks like you pissed yourself."

"Shit, really?"

"Yeah..."

"I think you guys should go."

They didn't argue.

THE BOY AT NO. 9 WHITLOCK

After they were gone, Matthew limped into the bathroom, intending to clean himself. Instead, he climbed into the empty tub and laid there in silence until sleep took him.

Chapter Seven

Unfortunately for Matthew, the aftermath of what Gordon had done to him that day was apparent to everyone that laid eyes on him. He felt it in the gaze of his neighbors as he walked down Whitlock. He felt it in the stares of the other passengers as he rode the late bus. He felt it in the gawks of his fellow students as he hobbled along the halls at school. He was marked. Damaged.

Of course, none of those who witnessed the boy's pained posture were more concerned than Christopher Hull.

"Okay Matthew, so, is there anything in particular you'd like to talk about during our session this afternoon?" the school counselor began. "Something you'd like to tell me?"

Unsurprised, he observed as Matthew responded the way he always did, by completely ignoring his questions as he stared out into the empty courtyard.

"I couldn't help but notice the way you've been carrying yourself today," he said frankly. "I gotta say, that looks pretty painful. Did you get into some kind of accident?"

"Sure," the boy said quickly.

"Would you like to tell me what ha–"

"I fell, okay!" the boy cut him off even quicker.

"Okay," Hull held up his hands. "Gotcha."

The counselor gently drummed the underside of his desk as he gathered his thoughts. This was the most Matthew had spoken with him since their appointments began six weeks ago. He knew from his short answers that he was not ready to talk about what really happened. If he wanted to keep him talking, he would have to navigate things more delicately.

"The school dance is on Friday," Hull mentioned casually. "What are your thoughts on that? Are you thinking of going?"

Matthew looked at the counselor for the first time in their allotted hour, and then his eyes returned to the window. The boy let out a long sigh.

"I've been having dreams about the woods," he told him.

"The woods?" Hull opened his notebook, pen at the ready.

"Where they found my brother," the boy clarified with a peeved scowl before he went on. "I see him there, where me and my friends go to mess around on the rope swings. Except he's not there to play. He's alone. He's standing on the edge, looking down at the stream. Then he looks up, and my mom is there, just floating over the water. She starts calling to him, like she wants him to join her. He's so happy to see her. So he reaches out to her and steps off the edge. He starts to fall... And that's when I wake up."

"That sounds like an intense dream to have," the counselor remarked, "for anyone."

A small laugh escaped, but still Matthew chose to remain facing away.

"Do you think it means anything?"

The boy gave a shrug.

"Alright," Hull nodded as he rapidly tapped on a page of his notebook with the tip of his pen. "What do *you* think it means?"

He was met with a second shrug.

"Matthew, do you think your brother did what he did so that he could be with your mother?"

Fully expecting a third shrug, it surprised Christopher Hull when a sad little voice from the other side of the desk replied, "Would that be so bad?"

THE BOY AT NO. 9 WHITLOCK
* * *

The lights were off in Heather's bedroom as she and Matthew sat beneath the covers, their eyes aglow from the glare of *Jaws* on VHS as they chowed down on a dinner plate's worth of PB&Js. Ricky was already passed out on the floor with his arms and legs spread out like a human starfish. His mouth hung wide open as he drooled onto the rug beneath him.

"So I actually talked to the school shrink today," Matthew told her.

"You mean, you gave him more than your one-word answer routine?" Heather joked.

"Yeah," he laughed.

"Good," she smiled at him. "I'm glad."

"I only did it because he was being weird," he said, taking another bite of his PB&J.

Heather paused the movie. "What do you mean by weird?

"He asked me if I was going to the dance on Friday," he replied reluctantly, embarrassed, his eyes clinging to the great white frozen on the TV screen.

"Oh, okay," Heather said curtly as she picked up the remote and pressed PLAY.

For a few uncertain moments, Matthew didn't know what to say or do. He had never seen her act like this before. Not only that, he was completely unfamiliar with this kind of behavior. Had he hurt her feelings? The very thought turned the bite of his sandwich into poison inside his mouth.

"So are you gonna ask me, or what?" she said so suddenly that the bed shook a little when she turned to face him.

He stuttered as he noticed she'd paused the movie again just to hear his answer.

"I don't fucking think so!" a voice exclaimed from below. Ricky sprang up into a superhero pose. "He promised to take *me* to the dance! So get in line, bitch! Now, come on and kiss me, Matty boy!"

They screamed as Ricky dove straight for them. The three of them rolled around in hysterics. Eyes watered, pillows flew and PB&Js were flattened amidst the mayhem.

"So we're all going together?" Heather asked breathlessly as she laid amongst their little pile of bodies.

* * *

With the help of Heather's mother, she and the boys arrived in full homemade costumes. Matthew's leather coat hit the floor as *The Crow*'s Eric Draven, while Ricky's plastic guns were confiscated the second he drew them as *Toy Story*'s Woody the cowboy, and Heather's locks were pinned away under a Mia Farrow pixie cut wig as she caressed the faux pregnant belly that carried *Rosemary's Baby*.

As they skirted around the overcrowded dancefloor with their bottles of soda, they quickly realized that the other attendants were mostly a who's who of Disney princesses, Universal Studios monsters and '80s slasher movie icons.

Curtained by darkness, the gymnasium was like a pool of tortured souls writhing about in the rising smoke. The piercing disco lights cast a ghoulish glow over everything as a sickly-sweet selection of dance-pop numbers from the last decade haunted their ears.

"Hope you guys are having a good time tonight!" the DJ's voice rang out over the closing seconds of the current track. "If you got a request just pass me a note with your song choice and if I got it, I'll play it!"

"Anybody got a request?" Ricky volunteered.

"Uh...Green Day?" Matthew suggested.

"Yes!" Ricky's eyes lit up. "Hold this for me!" Handing over his soda, he turned and waded into the crowd.

"Don't forget," the DJ's voice came again, "for just one dollar you can buy a rose for your date. You got a girlfriend? Or a boyfriend? Or maybe you got a secret crush? Make someone feel special and get them a rose. If you're feeling the love tonight, it's worth every cent because it's all for a good cause!"

"Aw, that's cute," Heather remarked, rubbing her large, round belly.

Matthew forced out a laugh, grinning like a chimp as he suddenly wanted to be anywhere else in that moment. Just then, he caught sight of Ricky motioning him towards the door.

"I'll be back in a sec, alright," he told Heather, heading for the exit before she could reply.

Matthew found Ricky standing at the end of the hall, beckoning for him to follow him round the corner to where the student lockers were.

Once he decided that Ricky had led him far enough, Matthew tapped his friend on the shoulder. "So what's up?"

"Man, take that dumb thing off," Ricky chuckled, "it makes you look like a girl."

"Shut up, *Woody*," Matthew grunted as he snatched off his own wig. "Come on, what is it? What are we doing out here?"

"We're here 'cause I got something to tell you," his friend said as he bowed his head, took off his hat and held it against his chest.

Matthew watched in silence as the cowboy reached under the hat and revealed to him a rose.

"Got it while you weren't looking," Ricky told him.

"For Heather?" Matthew frowned, his mouth suddenly dry as he regretted his initial reluctance at the idea.

"No." Ricky said as he presented it to him.

"For me?" Matthew's eyes narrowed in their confusion.

"Yeah." Ricky nodded as he bit his lower lip softly. "So... What do you think?"

"But I thought you liked Heather..."

Ricky shook his head. "Nope."

"But you're always there doing that thing where you're, you know, you're always trying to stop me from—"

"I wasn't doing it to you," Ricky explained. "Heather likes you, Matty. I wasn't trying to stop you. I was trying to stop her. Because...I like you, too."

"Boys," a man's voice startled them.

They turned to find Christopher Hull standing only a few lockers away.

"You shouldn't be out here," Hull warned them. "Come on now, get back to the dance. Unless you'd like to leave early?"

"Yes, sir!" Ricky squeaked as he wasted no time in scurrying past him back to the gymnasium with Matthew following close behind.

"Matthew?"

The boy stopped and looked back at the school counselor.

"I can keep a secret," Hull reminded him.

Matthew's eyes fell as they spotted the rose on the ground behind him, realizing that Ricky must have dropped it there when they got caught. He didn't dare ask to go back for it, so all he could do was acknowledge Hull's words with a nod and go on his way.

Back at the dance, he approached Heather and Ricky with a warm smile and handed each of them a rose.

"For you guys!" he screamed over the music.

"Aw, what you do that for?" Heather beamed.

"'Cause you guys are the best!" Matthew replied, winking at Ricky who smiled back at him in return.

The sound of Billie Joe Armstrong's guitar/vocals filled the air.

"They're playing our song!" Ricky shrieked with joy as their trio linked hands and started jumping to Green Day's 'Basket Case'.

* * *

Later that night, Heather walked Matthew home, his skin still drying from washing off the black and white face paint of his Halloween costume.

"So, tonight was amazing," Heather said with a big sigh as she sat down on his front stoop.

"Tonight was fun," Matthew agreed, sitting down next to her.

"Celebrate with me," she invited him as she held out an open pack of smokes.

"Your mom's?" he asked as she passed him a cigarette.

"Uh-huh," Heather nodded with a proud giggle. "Stole them from her glove compartment."

The two each took turns lighting the other up. And then, as they leaned back against the door to No. 9 Whitlock, they took their first drag and gazed up at the stars.

Heather enjoyed the sound of their village at this late hour until her gaze fell upon the person sitting next to her. There was so much that she wanted to say to him. But what could she say to a boy like Matthew?

She rested her head on his shoulder as a tear fell from her eye. Pulling down the end of her sleeve to clean up the spot where her teardrop fell, she looked down to find a familiar handle peering out of his pants pocket. She grabbed the knife, pushing herself away from him in her shock.

"Matt!" She showed him the blade. "Did you have this on you the whole night?"

Matthew gave the knife a mere glance before he took another drag.

Heather did her best to hold her hard stare, but when the reply she was waiting for didn't come, she ripped up her sleeve and held the blade to her arm.

Matthew's eyes grew wide. "What are you doing?"

Although her tears had returned, Heather said nothing.

Matthew put down his cigarette and reached out to her. "I'm sorry. I shouldn't have done that. It was stupid."

"Really stupid," she nodded, sniffing. "And dangerous."

"That too," he nodded back. "I'm sorry, okay. I'm sorry. I won't do it again, I swear."

Heather lowered her head as she took the blade away from her arm, wishing that she could believe his promise. "I should throw this away right now..."

Suddenly, the front door yanked open behind them. Matthew snatched the knife out of her hand and out of Gordon's sight as he filled the doorway.

"Hello, Matthew," he said through a vanishing smile as he grabbed his son by the back of his collar and threw him into the house with chilling ease.

It all happened too fast for Heather to protest.

"Goodnight!" Gordon smiled again, slamming the door in her face.

Flustered and frightened, she gathered up her mother's things and made a run for home.

The far wall of the hallway cracked under Matthew's body as Gordon sent him stumbling into it with a single shove.

"Where fuck you been?" the man boiled with his usual drunken dialect. "Always sneakin' out. Know you not allowed out after dark."

"I went to the dance, okay!" the boy told him. "With my friends."

"Who?" Gordon croaked.

"My *best* friends, Heather and Ric–"

"Ha! Don't have friends!" Gordon hooted. "Just a weirdo fag 'n a bitch feel sorry for you."

"At least I'm not alone like you," his son fired back. "Mom's dead, I fucking hate you, and Eric probably killed himself to get the fuck away from you!"

The floor shook beneath his feet as his father stomped towards him and punched him in the throat. The boy wheezed and gasped for air as his neck throbbed and ached. In a breathless panic, he drew the blade concealed in his back pants pocket and charged.

Gordon smashed him into the floor. His nose and lips bled as he laid there groaning. He tried to roll himself over, but the knife slipped from his grip and into his father's view.

"You trynna kill me?" He stamped on the boy's hand first. "Ya lil' fucker!"

Then, without hesitation or remorse, he kicked Matthew in the temple.

The boy stopped moving after that.

Chapter Eight

The bathroom was dark and silent as Matthew's body lay unconscious in the tub. His arms were placed in a cross over his chest as he slept there, so peacefully.

There was a click. A moment later, the lights flickered on. Then came a squeal of metal as the cold tap turned by itself. The hum of rushing water echoed against the stone-gray tiled walls.

A freezing puddle quickly formed around the boy's toes. It spread fast along the base of the tub until it pooled around his body.

Matthew gasped awake, eyes wide and searching. He felt the side of his head, expecting to graze against a protruding mass of tender flesh, only to find nothing, not even a bruise. Shivering, he sat up, turned off the water and opened the drain.

As the pipes gargled away beneath him, he gazed up at the window to find that it was still nighttime outside. Even so, he had no idea how many hours had passed, or how he got there.

The boy jolted at a sudden sharp cracking noise, like the sound of bones snapping. Barely able to grip the side of the tub, he held his breath as he scanned the room.

"Hello?" he said.

The tub creaked as he dropped his head the second he uttered the word, cursing himself for ever letting it past his lips. He shut his eyes tight and prayed that his father had not heard him speak.

But there was no one there. No one's footsteps in the hall or climbing the stairs. No one's hand rapping on the door or trying the handle.

Then, something in the air changed. The smell of rotting fruit and burnt paper filled his nostrils and clung to the back of his throat.

There was something else in that room with him. He could feel its presence towering over him. It was standing at the edge of the tub looking down at him. It was just as tall as he remembered, and its eyes, just as haunting.

Whatever the thing was, it was not a physical being. To look upon its form was like peering through a finely woven veil. Still, the boy had no doubt that it was there.

"Hello, Matthew," it said with a deep purr. "I'm sorry for frightening you during our first encounter. I can assure you that I'm not here to harm you. As a matter of fact, I'm here to make sure that no one harms you ever again."

The boy could barely bring himself to speak, and yet he begged the question, "Why? I mean- Why me?"

"I heard the pain in your soul as it cried out for help," it told him. "And then I saw the path of your existence, marked with the scars of those that have tormented you. There is a balance to everything, and I am here to punish those who punish others."

"So, you brought me up here?" Matthew asked as he looked around the tub.

"Yes."

He pointed to his unblemished temple. "And you fixed this?"

"Among other things," it said.

"What do you mean?" he asked it as he clutched the side of the tub. "What did you do?"

"Matthew..."

"Tell me, please," the boy demanded.

"You must understand," it said as it tried to calm him. "This man would see you dead now, given the choice."

"You hurt my dad?" Matthew was surprised at the concern in his own voice.

"Your father's punishment has already begun."

"Where is he?" Matthew raised his voice as he raised himself out of that tub. "What did you do to him?"

"If you'll follow me, I will show you," it said as the bathroom door unlocked and opened itself.

In motion, the veiled one was but a faint blur as it left the room.

Once it was out of sight, Matthew climbed out of the bathtub and reluctantly stepped out onto an empty landing.

"Where are you?" he called out.

He heard a door click open downstairs.

"He's in the living room," a voice as clear as winter rain spoke into his ear.

Matthew wasted no time in descending the stairs, but when he reached the very last step he stopped to take a breath.

Was this going to be the last time he would ever see his father? He didn't know. Despite everything that had happened between them, for better or worse, he was the only family he had left.

Believing himself to be ready, he placed an unsteady hand upon the doorframe and walked in.

And then he saw his father.

Gordon Rose was standing in the center of the room, his back to the TV. His face was frozen in agony as his mouth hung agape, his trembling eyes rupturing vessel after vessel as they bulged out of their sockets. Deep creases grew upon his body, splitting and bleeding as his skin was stretched inhumanely taut from behind by a force yet to make itself known. It made a rapid squelching noise that was unrelenting, like the sound of a large dog lapping up a bowl of water with its huge tongue.

Matthew kept a safe distance from the man as he slowly walked around him in search of the source. He stopped still with a gasp as he caught sight of something coming out of the TV. Whatever it was, it was latched onto his father's back, feeding off of him.

The cables that ran between man and machine bore the slippery translucency of worm flesh. Scaly and pulsating, they pumped slithers of Gordon's organ meat from his juddering torso into the back of the old television set. Already a quarter full of the man's shredded innards, the hollow glass box inside was like a vivarium of gore.

"Jesus..." the boy said as he marveled at the sight before him in horrified wonder. "Is he...dead?"

"There is no reversing his punishment," the voice said simply. "Do you want it to stop?"

Matthew failed to respond at first, distracted by his father's stomach as it began to cave in on itself.

"His torment fascinates you," the voice said with a pleased purr.

"I've always been the one getting hit," he told it. "Never knew what it was like to be the other one."

"And how does it feel?"

"It feels..." Matthew shook his head. "But I don't want to hurt anybody."

"You're not," it reassured him. "*I am.*"

The boy felt its long fingers as they curled around his shoulders and squeezed them comfortingly.

"You don't need him anymore," it whispered softly. "I'm here for you now."

Matthew thoughtfully pulled himself away, caressing one of its fingers as he went. He stepped slowly around the sickening spectacle that his father had become until they were face to face.

"You ruined my life," he said, his body tremoring with years of pain and anger. "Mom, Eric. You ruined all our lives. The funny thing is I almost feel sorry for you right now. But this... *This* is exactly what you deserve. I'm glad you suffered before you died. I'm glad it hurts. Maybe now you'll know. Ha... I'm just sorry I wasn't the one to do it. So fuck you, Dad. Fuck you for everything. *Fuck you.*"

Stepping away, Matthew exhaled deeply, feeling the weight of all his hurt expel from his body, a soul finally unburdened. He dried his eyes, wiping away the last of what little tears he had left to cry for his father.

A yellowish-white gunk splattered against the side of the glass box as the macabre contraption had liquefied the man's bones down to a pale purée. A thick, slimy sheen now coated him as if he had been submerged in a vat of saliva.

"So...is this what you do to all of them?" Matthew asked.

"I'll do whatever you ask of me," it said.

With nothing solid left in him, his father's body began to break down at an alarming rate. His features ran together like wet paint. His hands shrank away until the skin hung loose and flailing like used medical gloves. His head, torso, and limbs collapsed inward as everything sank onto the carpet in one steaming mound of human goop.

Gordon's punishment was complete.

"Now sleep, dear Matthew." The voice swam inside the boy's head as veiled hands lowered him into his father's armchair. "I will take care of everything."

When he awoke in the early hours the following morning, all of his father's human remains were gone. Every last trace. There was nothing left of him. It was as if Gordon Rose had never existed.

Chapter Nine

They had not been back to the woods since Eric died.

It no longer felt like the same place to them anymore. It certainly didn't look the same. The hand of fall had waved away most of the greenery, and the stream that ran through it all overflowed from the excess of fallen leaves.

The swing where it happened was now just a lonely, frayed rope, swinging silently in the autumn breeze.

Matthew and Ricky stood upon the roots of the tree it was tethered to, gazing out at it as they realized that they would never swing from it again. A part of their childhood had died along with Eric that day.

It then occurred to Matthew that changes like these were a part of what makes a person grow up. Every once in a while something came along that urged you to move on from the good things in life. And you can never go back because the things that made life good in the first place just aren't there anymore.

He figured that everyone was allotted a certain amount of happiness. And then life starts to chip away at it. Suffering under his father's guardianship, the pieces were subtle and small, but every now and then life took a big piece. For Matthew, Eric was his last big piece.

"You okay?" Ricky asked.

His best friend's shoulders sank as he let out a deflated sigh. "I thought if I came here I would – I don't know – feel him, you know?"

"You really think he'd wanna come out *here*?" Ricky said doubtfully.

"Guess not." Matthew bit his lower lip in thought. "Things have been kind of weird at the house since..."

"Weird? Like, how weird?"

"Like, really weird."

"Like, *oh...my...god!*" Ricky said in a valley girl voice.

"Shut up." Matthew punched him in the shoulder as he couldn't help but laugh. "Come on, let's check out the treehouse."

"Do we have to..." Ricky whined, his eyes following him as he climbed down towards the edge of the stream.

Matthew stood at the bottom of the rope ladder, holding it steady for Ricky while he cautiously made his climb.

"Keep it still!" he shouted down.

"I am!" Matthew shouted up.

"I'd love to know whose brilliant idea it was to build a treehouse right where the farmer can see us and fucking shoot us!"

There wasn't much Matthew could say to that. After all, Ricky was right.

Eric and his friends had built the house at the very edge of the woods, right on the treeline. The tree *itself* was an entrance! It even had a stile post nailed to its trunk to help ramblers over the stone wall that divided woodland from farmland.

They were certainly exposed. Especially since Farmer Mary always harvested her crop early to avoid frost damage, should the cruel subzero temperatures of a bitter winter arrive sooner than expected. The land was now bare, and the soil would sleep until springtime came around once again.

The sheer sturdiness of the structure never failed to impress them as they tested each room with their feet before they entered. The two boys stood in what remained of the bedroom space of the treehouse.

Stability aside, the room was but an empty wooden box with a raised platform in one corner and a lopsided window in the other.

"Can't believe kids used to come and sleep in here," Ricky remarked, holding out his hands for balance he didn't need as he walked over to the sawn out window.

"That's what happened," Matthew told him as he sat down on the bed. "Eric and Dad fought all the time. So, whenever he ran away, he wouldn't go to a friend's house. Eric came here. Probably spent more time here than anyone else."

Ricky sat down next to him. "Do you feel him, here?"

Matthew looked around intently as Ricky leaned in.

"No, I don't think so. Mm–" He paused as his friend kissed him. Surprised, he got to his feet and headed for the jagged doorway.

"Matty..." Ricky sprang from the bed to give chase when Matthew turned back to him.

"Can we go to your place and play videogames or something?" he asked, smiling through tears. "I don't think I want to hang out here anymore."

"Sure." Ricky nodded in his relief. "Sure. Whatever. Let's get the fuck out of here before that crazy ol' bitch shoots one of us in the ass."

Matthew shook with laughter as he dried his eyes with the back of his hand.

"Thank you for coming out here with me," he said as he found himself back at the bottom of the rope ladder, this time, waiting for his nervous friend to make his way down.

"Yeah, well, one of us had to be the super brave one," Ricky replied, already breathless from his descent.

As he took his last step off the ladder, his best friend enveloped him in a hug.

"Things really have been weird at the house," Matthew whispered, fingers pressing deeply.

Ricky opened his mouth to speak when Symes leapt from the stone wall, swinging a full bottle of vodka.

"Why you hittin' yourself!" he cheered as it socked off the back of Matthew's skull with a loud *CLINK!* His body locked up as he toppled to the ground hard. He lay there rigid in the dirt as Wayne appeared behind Ricky. The older kid yanked Ricky's shirt up over his face, trapping his arms behind his head.

Symes ignored his muffled protests as he unscrewed the cap off the bottle.

"Hey, I thought we were gonna drink that!" Wayne puzzled as Ricky thrashed left and right.

"We will." Symes grinned as he poured the vodka down the boy's exposed chest and belly. "This is just to make it hurt more!"

Symes took a swig before he stumbled over to his buddy.

"Here ya go, babe," he hummed as he tipped a mouthful down Wayne's throat.

They kissed.

And then he repositioned himself in front of Ricky as he took off his belt.

"Hold him still!" he ordered as he raised it high.

The afternoon air echoed with wet *SNAP!* after wet *SNAP!* of the belt lashing Ricky's bare, vodka-soaked skin. All the while he screamed for his best friend to save him as his body streamed with blood from the deep welts that now plagued his torn flesh.

"What do ya say, psycho boy?" Symes called back over his shoulder as he spun the belt like a helicopter blade. "You gonna save him or what?"

"I don't think he's getting up anytime soon!" Wayne cackled as he pointed.

Symes turned and burst out laughing as he discovered Matthew convulsing on the ground behind him. Watching him with a sick fascination, he kicked at the boy as he quietly seized at his feet.

"What the fuck's going on?" Ricky cried out. "Leave him alone!"

"Shut the fuck up, nancy boy!" Symes sneered, setting the bottle down on the stile.

BLAM!

The thing exploded into a million shards, splashing vodka across his face. "Shit!"

"Stay right where you are!" a bellowing voice followed the gunshot. Fast approaching footsteps crunched over the cold soil.

Wayne pushed Ricky to the dirt as he and Symes made a run for it, their shadows stretching long into the low afternoon sun.

Mary marched out of the field, smoke still rising from the muzzle of her shotgun as she wore a pleased smirk above a thick rain jacket, mustard yellow scarf and faded jeans.

"You're alright," she reassured Ricky as she freed him from his tangled shirt and pulled him to his feet. "They won't be back."

"Matty!" Ricky gasped as he ran to his friend's side.

"Allow me," Mary said, motioning him away with a tilt of the head.

She gently placed her hand upon Matthew's forehead, like a mother checking her sick child for a fever. And as if by miracle, through the farmer's touch, his seizures subsided.

The boy took in a breath and stirred as he slowly regained consciousness. His nose twitched to the smell of burnt paper, and the sound of bones snapping like twigs nearby.

"What happened?" he barely managed.

"You're going to be okay, young man." Mary smiled.

Her eyes rolled back white as she crouched down beside him. But it wasn't her face. Not really. Through his dizzy haze he saw another face, flesh rotted and eyes piercing, veiled over hers.

"I'm here, Matthew," its voice spoke through her, though her lips remained still. "I'm here for you."

* * *

The first thing that Wayne saw when he awoke was the tiny blob of meat sitting in the center of his chest as he lay beneath the bare treetops. At first he mistook the thing for a piece of raw chicken wing, until his vision came into full focus. The tiny blob had tiny legs, and a tiny face. It was then that he realized he was looking at a newborn hedgehog, a hoglet.

He gave the poor creature a grimace of disgust as he attempted to buck it off of his chest.

Something stung his arms as he tried to lift them. That's when he saw the barbed wire, dripping with blood. One end was coiled around his arm, from elbow to wrist. The other end was pinned down into the earth by a wooden fence post. There were three more posts hammered into the ground, each one holding one of his remaining limbs in place, their barbed teeth drawing more pain, more blood.

Wayne turned his head to the sound of someone whispering his name, and screamed.

Symes' body was swarming with hundreds of newborn hogs. Their limp little bodies were fused together over his, like a second skin. His mouth disappeared as a tide of lumpy flesh rolled over his face until only one eye remained. It blinked at Wayne one last time before it vanished beneath his new hog skin.

"Symes?" Wayne called out to him. "Symes!"

There was only silence as this new being lost its humanoid form, spreading out into a wide meaty puddle.

A hand burst out, reaching up blindly into the air. The hoglet flesh squelched as Symes' face broke through its surface, shrieking for help.

His frightened eyes ran red with blood, wounded by the countless quills that pierced his face and neck.

"I can't move!" Wayne cried, his mind flashing from one arm to the other, too afraid to pull himself free.

Symes disappeared with a whimper as the atrocity swallowed him whole a second time.

"Symes!" Wayne yelled as the puddle of hog meat began to shrink before his eyes.

He heard sickening snaps, and screams of agony. He saw ruptures of blood like bursting pustules. Then, all he heard was quiet as the mass had diminished into a sphere of oily flesh, no bigger than a pumpkin.

Wayne watched as the hoglets separated and dissolved, revealing what was left inside as they wasted away.

Symes was now nothing more than a blood-soaked ball of broken bones and quill infested skin. His punishment was complete.

* * *

"You're not going to need stitches," the young nurse informed Ricky on completing her examination of his wounds. "But I am going to need to clean and dress these before I let you go. I will be right back with your dressings." She smiled sweetly as she breezed out of the treatment room.

Ricky sat frozen in a hunch upon the table, trying his best not to effect his injuries in any way.

"I'm so sorry, buddy," Matthew said soundly, his head bowed as he sat across from him in the visitor's chair. "This wouldn't have happened if I didn't make you go up there with me. What are you doing?"

"I'm tired!" Ricky yawned as he slowly laid himself down upon the paper towel on the examination table.

His body jolted as he winced in pain.

"Jeez, Ricky..." Matthew reached out to comfort his friend, mindful of touching his open skin. "Be careful, will ya!"

Scrunching his eyes shut, Ricky clenched his teeth as he bore his way through it.

"Matty..." he groaned soundly.

"Yeah?"

"I've got something to tell you," Ricky said woozily as a tear rolled off the side of his nose.

"What is it?" Matthew asked, edging his chair closer.

"It's all my fault." Ricky smiled dumbly.

"What are you talking about? What's all your fault?"

"I'm the snitch," Ricky confessed as his eyes finally closed. "I'm the one who snitched on Symes. I thought I could get him suspended, so we wouldn't have to deal with him at school for a while. But...it didn't work. Nobody did anything about it. And now look at me. So that fucking backfired..."

"You think!" Matthew remarked with a sarcastic huff.

"I'm sorry, Matty." Ricky yawned again.

"Ah, don't worry about it." Matthew checked the open doorway before he moved his chair even closer. "Besides, I don't think we need to worry about those guys messing with us anymore."

"What makes you say that?" Ricky was drifting. His body dripped with tainted blood as his wounds had already begun to weep.

"Ricky?" Matthew placed a hand upon his ankle. "There's something I need to tell you too."

His friend hummed in response.

"...I think Wayne and Symes are going to di–"

"Sorry about that," the young nurse said as she glided back into the room with a tray full of supplies.

The roll tore as Ricky shot upright, the exam paper clinging to his wet injuries.

Meanwhile, Matthew shut his mouth up tight and backed away from the table.

"I hope you're a brave kid," the nurse said as she lifted a wet paper towel from a bowl of sterile water, "because this is going to sting a little."

* * *

Tears streaming down his trembling cheeks, Wayne turned his gaze away from Symes' remains. He choked out a scream of horror as he found a frenzied mass wriggling its way up his belly.

Then his chest.

Then his throat.

And finally, his head.

He felt a thousand quills sinking into him as it devoured everything. He tasted blood from his lungs amidst the suffocating darkness that encapsulated him.

With no way out, he could only hope that he drowned first before his fleshy cocoon crushed him down into a little ball of mangled nothing.

Chapter Ten

Matthew wore the best shirt he owned as he waited on the curb outside Heather's house with a pile of stones in his hand. One by one, he threw them at her window until she appeared behind the sunset-tinged glass.

Pulling it open, she leaned her head out with a smile.

"Why are you dressed like that?" she asked him.

"Dressed like what?" He blushed coyly. "I'm going somewhere. Wanna come with me?"

"Sure," she said. "Should I put on something nice?"

"If you want to," he shrugged. "I don't mind."

She soon appeared at her door in a flowy dress, too fine for the November weather, but she didn't care.

Even so, Matthew made sure to drape her shoulders with his jacket before he picked his bike up off the street and showed her to her seat. Mounting the pedals, he double-checked that she was secure, placing her hands firmly upon his hips.

"Hold on to me," he told her with a wink as he started to cycle along Whitlock. "Don't let go."

"I won't," she promised.

There was nothing like gliding down a clear road on your bike to make you feel like you were flying when you were a kid. Arms spread, wind rushing at your face at what felt like a hundred miles an hour. That feeling of invincibility, of immortality...of peace.

Heather held Matthew's jacket high over her head and closed her eyes as she took it all in. Homes flashed by like lost photographs. People became a blur like faded memories. And soon streets and sidewalks gave way to trees and stone walls.

A couple of near accidents and one shaky climb later, Heather found herself standing in a dark, creaking doorway, patiently waiting as she wore a loose-fitting blindfold.

"Almost ready," the nervous boy's voice assured her as she listened to a hushed commotion of shuffling, thumping and cursing.

"Okay," the girl giggled in her excitement.

She could feel the warmth of him as he appeared in front of her, taking her hands in his.

"This way," he said, guiding her into the room until they were sitting next to one another. "You can take it off now."

Heather did as she was told, and when the blindfold came away she found herself in the bedroom of Eric's treehouse. There were burning candles of all sizes hanging from the ceiling and glass jars filled with flowers on the floor.

"My brother and his buddies used to bring their girlfriends here whenever they wanted to be alone," Matthew explained as he looked around the room with pride. "He told me he had a lot of special times here."

Heather looked at the candles, the flowers, and then at Matthew as she braced herself to speak.

"So..." she began with a long sigh, "you thought it would be romantic to take me out to see your brother's fuck hut?"

The second she said it, the two of them burst out laughing.

"Oh my god." Matthew's head hung low with embarrassment. "This was the worst idea ever!"

"Aw, no," Heather tried to reassure him. "It's actually kinda sweet."

"Really?" he asked with a hopeful gaze.

"No, it's not," she cringed. "It's totally gross!"

"Ah, shit!" he groaned, kicking over a jar of daffodils.

"But it was nice that you tried," she said soothingly as she took his hand. "Thank you, Matt."

"You're welcome, Heather," he smiled.

She gave him a long hug and finished it with a peck on the cheek.

"I thought you said you were never coming back here!" Ricky fumed from the doorway. "Guess you didn't want me to know about this, you fucking asshole!"

"Ricky!" Matthew called to him, but when he got to his feet his friend was gone.

By the time he reached the outside, Ricky had thrown himself from the treehouse and was already limping his way across the field, as fast and as far away from him as he could manage.

"Goddamn it, Ricky."

* * *

Ricky found the gas can in the garage, red with a black screw cap. It wouldn't fit in his backpack, so he carried it out there by hand.

For the first time, he climbed that rope ladder without assistance or fear. And when he reached the top he didn't hesitate once as he doused each room in fuel. All except one.

He took a pause in the bedroom as he recalled the afternoon that he kissed Matthew. But as the thought occurred to him that Matthew would never kiss him back, he made sure to cover every inch of that room in gasoline.

Before he knew it, he was standing back on the ground with the can by his feet as he watched Eric's treehouse burn, the flames hypnotic as they danced against the dark morning sky.

* * *

Matthew heard the sirens first in the early hours, fire trucks racing through the village. Then he got a call from Heather around breakfast time. Someone had burned down the treehouse. He couldn't believe it. He had to see it for himself. She wanted to go with him, but he insisted that this was something he needed to do on his own.

The house was a charred ruin. Its walls had fallen in on each other like a toppled house of cards. Smoke still rose from some places, water still dripped from others. The stile at its trunk was wrapped in yellow and black barrier tape, and the soil surrounding its roots had become a large muddy pond. Even the rope ladder was gone, leaving him unable to get up there and sift through the wreckage.

"Fuck," Matthew sobbed as he kicked a piece of debris.

"You know who did this," said the voice.

"What are you still doing here?" Matthew asked it. "I thought we were done?"

"I'm here to carry out punishment," it replied.

"No way, he's my best friend," the boy said firmly. "This is my fault. He's just mad at me because I made him jealous. *I* did this. *I* hurt *him*. I don't hate him."

"Dear Matthew," it purred wickedly. "That is no longer any concern of mine. Remember, I told you everything has a balance, and I am here to punish those who punish others. All three of your tormentors were punished on your behalf. So now the balance demands that you yourself be punished...in the taking of all those you hold closest to your guilty beating heart."

"The fuck you will!" Matthew yelled as he squared up to the tall, rotting shadow. "I didn't agree to any of this! And I sure as shit never asked you to kill anybody!"

"But you did," it told him. "You forget, I can hear your soul."

"My soul doesn't want this!" Matthew fired back.

"You know a punishment cannot be reversed," it reminded him.

"Punishment?" The boy stumbled as he lost the fight in his voice. "No... No, no, no. You didn't... What did you do?"

*

The side entrance to the building was waiting open for him when he arrived at the high school. There was no broken glass, no forced lock, but the alarm circuit had been disconnected.

There was something deeply unnatural about the empty quiet of that place as Matthew walked down the corridor towards the lockers. But there was no one there.

A ghostly breath blew through the idling door, rapping against the entrance to the school gym behind him. Of course, the place where he and Ricky had danced together hand in hand.

It was dark inside the gymnasium when Matthew hauled its doors open. He froze as the rush of air echoed throughout the vast hall like the wings of a great bird making flight.

Taking his first few steps inside, he called out his friend's name, but that first attempt was simply too weak for his voice to carry through the heavy shadows of that deep room.

The morning sky's pale glow shone through the glass of the emergency exit, granting him just enough visibility to make out his surroundings. The crepe streamers from the Halloween disco still hung from the walls in orange, black, and purple. They rippled in the breeze like paper tentacles as Matthew walked by them.

"Come on, where is he?" he called out as he refused to take another step. "I swear to God if you–"

Words failed him as the spotlights snapped on to reveal the thing waiting for him in the center of that room.

"Jesus, Ricky..." Matthew gasped under his breath as he marveled at the grisly sight, frozen with horror.

His legs were nothing but bare bone, twisted together into one long, lean stem. His torso was horribly emaciated. Thinning soft tissue clung to every rib. The arms were spread wide as his dancing fingers wore leaves of skin delicately flayed from his own wrists. Ricky smiled madly through the agony as the meat around his face was peeled forward and separated as it bloomed out into five tear-shaped petals of bloodied flesh. The demon had carved his friend into a flower, a human rose.

"Matty..." Ricky cried as his stem of bones began to splinter.

"I'm here," Matthew soothed him as he wilted into his arms.

"I don't know what happened." Ricky could barely breathe as he wept tears of blood. "Everything hurts."

But Ricky's tears were not tears at all. Under the strain of his barbaric transformation, his face was slowly splitting apart. It wouldn't be long until it was just as open and raw as the rest of his mutilated body.

"I can't see," he shivered with fear. "Am I dying?"

It was in that moment that Matthew realized this was going to be the last time he would ever see his best friend. The boy who loved him laid dying in his arms, never to feel another boy's love in return. And so, he lifted him up and he held him. He held him with every bit of love that Gordon never gave him. With every bit of love that he will never give to Eric. And with every bit of love that Ricky deserved, unconditionally, from Matthew himself.

As their embrace ended, so did Ricky's suffering. His blood-pooled eyes stared lifelessly into the lights high above them. His punishment was complete.

"Ricky... No..." Matthew wailed as his entire body shook with grief. "Please don't leave me..."

Leaning into him, he finally gave his friend the kiss he had always wanted.

But it was one kiss too late.

Matthew laid Ricky gently down and bowed his head as silence fell in the darkness of the gymnasium.

Suddenly, the great room exploded with light as the alarm system blared throughout the school.

Matthew gasped with a chill of realization.

"Heather..."

Rising to his feet, he looked upon his friend for the final time. And with that, he turned and ran for the exit.

Chapter Eleven

For two whole blocks Matthew fought to close his coat and hide the stains of Ricky's blood on his shirt, but his hands were shaking so hard he could barely get a grip on the tiny zipper.

His face was ice cold, his cheeks like two thick slabs of numb meat, frozen by his own tears.

Two sharp horn blasts jolted him to a standstill.

"Fuck..."

He hadn't noticed the vehicle that had been silently following him down the block for the past minute, not until the driver made himself known and pulled up alongside him.

"Mr. Hull?"

There was simply no time to compose himself, no time to feign normality. Even as he tried to palm away the sadness from his face, it occurred to him, maybe this was his normality.

"Matthew, how are you?" Christopher Hull asked the boy as he wound his window down. "You missed your last appointment with me. I was concerned."

"I'm fine," Matthew stammered. "I mean... I'm not okay. But I'm getting help. My...my friend's aunt is a therapist. I'm... I'm on my way there now, actually, to see... her."

"You're on your way there now?" Hull leaned on the car door as he spoke. "Well, why don't I give you a ride? I mean, you look like your catching a cold already. It'd be no trouble. What do you say?"

Keeping his bloodied hands concealed within his coat sleeves, Matthew got into the school counselor's vehicle and gave him the directions to Heather's Aunt Sheila's place.

It was a relatively quiet car journey, much to the boy's relief. Until they came to a stop at the end of Sheila's street.

"I've been trying to get in touch with your dad for a few days now, but he hasn't returned any of my calls," Hull informed him. "Could you maybe let him know that I'm looking to talk to him? Get him to call me back? If there's a problem, I could pay you both a visit sometime."

"Please don't do that," Matthew said firmly. "Don't come to my house. He doesn't wanna talk to you...sir..."

Aghast, the counselor's jaw hung slightly ajar.

Certain that Hull would say nothing more, Matthew thanked him for the ride and got out of the car. After he shut that passenger door he didn't look back.

"Please be there. Please be there."

Matthew uttered the prayer so many times on his march up the street to Heather's Aunt Sheila that he could feel the words throb along to the beat of his own pounding heart.

"Please be there. Please be there."

The prayer vanished beneath his breath when Sheila's front door swung inward on the first knock. It just opened so easily, giving no fight or resistance, not even from a latch.

Knuckles stilled at mid-knock, the boy recoiled by half a backstep as the hallway before him brimmed with gray smoke.

"Sheila?" Matthew called out as he ran inside.

But there couldn't be any fire. There was no overwhelming heat, no growing thunder of hungry flame.

Her name caught in his mouth on his turn to enter the living room. He grasped the wooden frame as he dared not pass the doorway to where the woman knelt upon the carpet.

THE BOY AT NO. 9 WHITLOCK

If she had a wise word to give him, she could not speak it, for her gaping mouth was ablaze with two hundred sticks of burning incense. Her body was riddled with them as they pierced forth from her flowery gown like thorns, each one deep enough to tease the surface of her bones.

The book that Matthew had stolen from her lay at her kneecaps. It twitched this way and that as its scaled faux-leather cover creaked and tore open. The five-pointed star lifted out of it, shifting composition from ink into gold metal, a blade in pentagram form.

As it climbed the air, the blade grew until it was great enough in size to lock Sheila's neck and wrists into place like a pillory. She gave a stifled wail as its razor edges sank into her skin.

"Let her go!" Matthew cried at the ceiling. "She's not my friend, or my family! She's nothing to me, so leave her alone!"

The demon's laugh purred in his ears. "Oh, dear father's son. Oh apple that rolls itself back to the tree. Witness a fragment of beautiful nothing."

And with those words, the star blade struck off the woman's head.

Matthew's grip tightened on the doorframe as he fought to remain conscious, the contents of his stomach bubbling up past his chest towards his throat. He forced his eyes shut and tried not to listen, but Sheila's arterial spray made a sound like raindrops falling heavily upon a car windshield as it pitter-pattered on his sneakers. Then came a scream. It was so inhuman, the boy had to look. He had to see what miscreation the demon had concocted now.

A great goat's head had emerged from the body's decapitated stump. Its horns were black and twisted, and its fur was stained red, soaked in the blood spilled afore its arrival as it heaved its sickly rotting fruit breath.

Its wild animal eyes locked on Matthew as the thing shrieked at him, frightening him back into the hallway. Sheila's body rose to its bare feet, grunting furiously, shoulders hunching forward, preparing to charge.

Matthew screamed as the goat-headed woman exploded across the room at him. He ran for the front door as she clawed at his jacket, tearing madly for his back. Surging forward, he leapt through the doorway out into the open air where he felt the creature's hands at him no longer. When he turned to look, Sheila's headless corpse lay sprawled over her stoop. The great horned beast was gone.

* * *

Matthew called out to Heather as he frantically thumped the glass of her front door with his fist.

Shapes moved behind the heavily tinted windowpane as someone approached. He leapt back as the handle turned sharply.

The face of Heather's mother appeared in the doorway, a frown of confusion contorting her handsome features.

"Matthew?" she uttered. "What are you doing here? Didn't Heather call on you? She left here about ten minutes ago."

"Ten minutes?" Matthew's eyes throbbed in a moment of panic before he collected himself. "Uh, yeah, that's right! Actually, we're just playing a game! Hide and Seek! Obviously, she's not here so... Thanks for your help!"

There was no time to hear her response as he turned and tore his way up the street towards No. 9 Whitlock.

He found Heather upstairs, sitting alone on his bed, her eyes rolled back white with a strange smile on her face.

"Welcome home, Matthew," she said with the demon's voice. "Behold, your final punishment. If you wish for me to leave you be, you must kill sweet, young Heather. If not, I will stay, and I will keep on killing...in the most delicious ways."

The girl let out a little chuckle as she held out Matthew's knife.

His eyes locked on the blade as he took it from her, raising it up so he could admire it. The knife his mother once used. He recalled the way she'd smile at him as he watched her use it. Just one of many memories that pierced through him like a heartless seamstress threading a needle repeatedly through his soul. The tears that felt like tears of blood that day he took the knife to himself somehow found him again.

"You know, just the other day I went to the place where Eric...died. And I was thinking that sometimes life takes – no, actually – it *rips* pieces of your happiness away from you until you got nothing left," Matthew told her, his tears bleeding down to the floor. "And I thought life ripped the last piece away from me when Eric left me here... But I was wrong. I still had you, and Ricky. My best friends. Every day I decided to keep going, it was because of you guys. But now Ricky's gone too... And it's my fault, I know that. But now you're all I have. *You* are my last piece, Heather. So please don't leave me like everyone else did. Please stay with me, okay? Stay with me."

A drop of sweat rolled its way down the side of Heather's face. Her hands trembled and her fingers curled. She let out a muffled squeal as one of her eyes strained itself forward, its blood vessels rising.

"The board!" she cried, forcing the words out through clenched teeth. "It's afraid of the board!"

"Shit, okay!" Matthew dropped to his knees and reached under the bed to where his father had kicked it. He dragged it out into the open. It still bore the scar above the five-pointed star he'd carved there with his blade.

"What do I do now?"

"Break the line!" Heather screamed. "Send it back!"

"Fuck it!" Matthew drew a breath and slammed the knife into the center of the line. Then he twisted it, splitting the ouiji board down the middle with a loud *CRACK!*

He let out a yelp as a great shadow appeared behind him.

The demon stood in the doorway of the boy's bedroom, taller than the doorway itself. The eyes that had haunted him from the first moment he saw them were wild with rage. Its long fingers scored the wood as it backed away, fading into the air until it was gone completely.

Matthew huffed out a great sigh as he fell over Heather's lap in his relief. He recoiled to his feet with a sharp gasp.

He stood frozen in disbelief as she lay there lifelessly upon the bed, her eyes returned but slowly sliding away on different paths as her pupils became widening pools of bottomless black.

*

The street was shrouded in nighttime as Heather found herself standing outside in the middle of the road on Whitlock. It was cold, and everything had that slick shine to it that could only be left by a heavy rain. There was something lurking at the end of the street. Something big. And it was floating towards her.

"Hello Heather," its voice was low and raspy, like a dying breath. "It's a pleasure to finally meet you."

The girl started to back away, inching herself further and further from the demon until just the right moment. And then she spun and ran...straight into Matthew!

"Matt!" she cried as she threw her arms around him. "How did you–"

"Come on, we gotta get you out of here." Taking her by the hand, he led her back up the street. "We just need to get you back to your body."

"And then what?" she asked, already breathless.

"I don't know," he laughed. "I've only ever done this solo, remember. I figure it'll work for you too."

Heather halted as they reached the bottom of Matthew's driveway.

"Wait... Who is that?" she said as she pointed at the man waiting on the front stoop. "I thought we were the only ones here?"

"I don't know." Matthew jogged up the drive towards him. "Aw, shit... It's Mr. Hull...the school shrink."

"What's he doing here?" Heather asked as she followed. "And what happened to him?"

Hull stood perfectly motionless at Matthew's front door. A statue made of flesh and bone, but with one glaring difference. His back and torso were teeming with demonic arms, their decayed cruelty bursting out of his body in droves, reaching through his innocent, kind-hearted skin with monstrous clawed fingers. In life, all that Christopher Hull's soul desired was to reach out and help others. And in the face of Matthew's veiled demon, reaching out finally became his undoing. Perhaps the most undeserving of all the punishments.

"He came over..." Matthew realized as he glanced at the agonized scream twisting up Hull's face. "I told him not to come over."

"Matt, I'm sorry, but we gotta keep going!" Heather pleaded, desperately patting at his back.

"Sorry!" he agreed, helping her move Hull's demon infested flesh statue aside.

They burst through the door of No. 9 Whitlock and raced up the staircase to Matthew's bedroom. But when they arrived it was empty.

"Where am I?" Heather puzzled with worry as she searched the room for herself. "I mean, is it supposed to be like this?"

"Relax," Matthew said softly, grasping her shoulders gently. "And just lie down in the spot where you were when it happened."

"Okay," she said as she gazed sadly into his eyes.

He took her hands. "So, you saw inside its head?"

"Yeah," she sighed, her bottom lip quivering.

"So you know about?"

"Ricky, yeah," she nodded, throwing her arms around him as she burst into tears.

"I didn't tell it to do that, I swear," he sobbed into her shoulder

"I know, I know," she reassured him, releasing him as she set to work drying her eyes and cleaning up her face.

"It used you. It never wanted to help you. It just wanted to hurt as many people as it could."

A shrill scraping sound came from behind them. They turned to find the demon levitating outside of Matthew's bedroom window, running the tips of its long fingers over the foggy pane.

Heather screamed as the glass suddenly lost its density, spilling over the windowsill and down the wall in a goopy, jelly like substance.

The demon smiled as it started to crawl into the room.

"You can't have her!" Matthew told it, holding strong as he stood between the demon and Heather.

"You gave her to me," it laughed as it relished in the truth of its words. And then its face changed. Its blackened, rotting flesh became brighter than morning snow as a blazing fiery light engulfed the room. "What is this?"

Matthew shielded his eyes as he turned to see where the illumination was coming from. What he saw stopped him. His hand fell by his side as everything inside his head fell silent.

Somehow this other reality had split in two as Matthew found himself peering into the dream he had described to Hull mere days ago. There his mother was, hovering over the stream where her eldest son, his brother, took his own life. But this time was different. This time Eric was by her side. Both of them looked happy. Radiant. Free from the horrors that life had cast upon them. They smiled at him knowingly as tears found their eyes.

The floor shook as the light emanating from them became brighter still. Flames began to dance across his mother's body. Something was building, growing, about to happen. Something dangerous, but something amazing.

Matthew pulled Heather to the floor as a great burst of energy surged over them. The entire bedroom wall disintegrated as its force blasted the demon far, far out into the night air until it vanished from sight somewhere over the city lights in the distance.

Opening his eyes, the boy looked up with just enough time to catch a final flicker of heavenly fire as his mother and brother, his family, his heart, his soul, vanished, returned to whatever paradise held them now.

Mom, he realized. *It was you from the start. You were the sun. I love you, Mom. I love you forever. I miss you so much.*

Heather held out her hand to him until he finally saw it, letting her help him to his feet.

"Let's get the hell out of here," she smiled.

"Good idea," he smiled back.

"Now would be a good time to have that kiss," she said, tugging playfully at his shirt.

"I'll kiss you on the other side." He squeezed her hand affectionately. "We better hurry."

"Okay," she agreed, laying back upon the bed. "Kiss you on the other side."

*

Heather shot upright from the bed as life breathed back into her body once again.

"Matt?" she called out as she looked around the room.

She noticed the ouiji board had moved, finding one broken half sitting in the open doorway. Getting up, she followed its direction out onto the landing.

The remaining half of the board was waiting for her outside the bathroom door.

"Matt?" This call was softer as she pushed the door slowly open.

She found Matthew's lifeless body lying in the tub.

"Oh Matt..." Heather held onto the handle as her grief anchored her aching soul down to the floor.

Even though he feared the pain, even though he feared the other side, without a single second of hesitation, he had opened his wrists for her. In his final moments, Matthew believed he deserved to be punished for everything that he had allowed to come to pass. Life took many pieces away from Matthew, but he couldn't let it take Heather, who was his last.

Perhaps, the greatest punishment of all was dying with the knowledge that she would always remember him as her first.

THE END

About The Author

L. Stephenson was born in Glasgow, Scotland, and has lived in the North-West of England for most of his life, where he graduated from university with a degree in Film & TV Screenwriting. His first short horror story was published in 2018, and three short years later came his first novella, *The Goners*. His debut novel, *The Boatmore Butcher* was released in 2023. Earlier that same year, his works also appeared in the Bram Stoker award–nominated anthology, *American Cannibal*. The following year, he curated his own Christmas horror anthology for charity, *Violent Advents*.

ALSO AVAILABLE BY THE AUTHOR:

When Strange Things Bite

The Boatmore Butcher (Dark Ink Books)

AUTHOR ALSO APPEARS IN:

Violent Advents: A Christmas Horror Anthology

Halloween Remains

American Cannibal (Maenad Press)

Unburied (Dark Ink Books)

Shadowy Natures (Dark Ink Books)

Ghosts, Goblins, Murder, & Madness (Dark Ink Books)

Horrorscope, Volume 3 (January Ember Press)

Born In A Black Cab (CAAB Publishing)

The Stuff of Nightmares (S.K. Gregory)